The Tiara Club

Also in the Tiara Club

Princess Charlotte *and the* Birthday Ball

Princess Katie *and the* Silver Pony

Princess Alice *and the* Magical Mirror

Princess Sophia *and the* Sparkling Surprise

Princess Emily *and the* Substitute Fairy

VIVIAN FRENCH

The Tiara Club

Princess Daisy
AND THE
Dazzling Dragon

ILLUSTRATED BY SARAH GIBB

KATHERINE TEGEN BOOKS
An Imprint of HarperCollins*Publishers*

Library of Congress Cataloging-in-Publication Data

French, Vivian.

Princess Daisy and the dazzling dragon / by Vivian French ;
illustrated by Sarah Gibb. — 1st U.S. ed

p. cm. — (The Tiara Club ; 3)

Summary: A timid young princess is afraid of dragons until
she sees one for herself, then has the opportunity to prove her
newfound courage to the entire school.

ISBN-10: 0-06-112434-6 (trade bdg.)

ISBN-13: 978-0-06-112434-1 (trade bdg.)

ISBN-10: 0-06-112433-8 (pbk.)

ISBN-13: 978-0-06-112433-4 (pbk.)

[1. Princesses—Fiction. 2. Courage—Fiction. 3. Dragons—
Fiction. 4. Schools—Fiction.] I. Gibb, Sarah, ill. II. Title.

PZ7.F88917Prid 2007   2006020331

[Fic]—dc22   CIP

                                                            AC

Typography by Amy Ryan

❖

First U.S. edition, 2007

The Royal Palace Academy
for the Preparation of Perfect Princesses
(Known to our students as "The Princess Academy")

OUR SCHOOL MOTTO:
A Perfect Princess always thinks of others before herself,
and is kind, caring, and truthful.

We offer the complete curriculum for all princesses, including:

How to Talk to a Dragon

Creative Cooking for Perfect Palace Parties

Wishes, and How to Use Them Wisely

Designing and Creating the Perfect Ball Gown

Avoiding Magical Mistakes

Descending a Staircase as if Floating on Air

Our principal, Queen Gloriana, is present at all times, and students are in the excellent care of the school Fairy Godmother.

VISITING TUTORS AND EXPERTS INCLUDE:

KING PERCIVAL *(Dragons)*

LADY VICTORIA *(Banquets)*

QUEEN MOTHER MATILDA *(Etiquette, Posture, and Poise)*

THE GRAND HIGH DUCHESS DELIA *(Fashion)*

We award tiara points to encourage
our princesses toward the next level.
Each princess who earns enough points
in her first year is welcomed to the
Tiara Club and presented with a silver tiara.

Tiara Club princesses are invited to return
next year to Silver Towers, our very special
residence for Perfect Princesses, where they
may continue their education at a higher level.

PLEASE NOTE:

Princesses are expected to arrive
at the Academy with a *minimum* of:

TWENTY BALL GOWNS
*(with all necessary hoops,
petticoats, etc.)*

TWELVE DAY-DRESSES

SEVEN GOWNS
*suitable for garden parties
and other special daytime
occasions*

TWELVE TIARAS

DANCING SHOES
five pairs

VELVET SLIPPERS
three pairs

RIDING BOOTS
two pairs

*Cloaks, muffs, stoles, gloves,
and other essential
accessories, as required*

Hello! And I really want to say hello to you the right way. Should I say, "Good day, Your Highness?" That doesn't sound very friendly, and I do want us to be friends. After all, we're at the Princess Academy together, aren't we? Oops! I nearly forgot to tell you— I'm Daisy! Princess Daisy. Have you met my other friends: Charlotte, Katie, Alice, Emily, and Sophia? They're learning to be Perfect Princesses, just like you and me. It's fun most of the time, but Princess Perfecta isn't very nice. We're really *really* happy that she doesn't share the Rose Room with us. She's much too mean!

Chapter One

Do you ever get scared of things? I do. For one thing, I'm scared I'll *never* get five hundred tiara points by the end of my first year here at the Academy, and then I won't be allowed to join the Tiara Club— and I really want to! It sounds so wonderful! And I'm scared of things like spiders and big, fierce dogs. Actually, thinking about *anything* big and fierce makes my knees weak! Our principal, Queen Gloriana, is scary too. She's very tall and gracious, but she can be very fierce if you do something wrong. Fairy Godmother—Fairy G.—is much friendlier, but even she can get angry. And when she does, she swells up to *twice* her usual size. Honestly. I'm not joking!

When I first heard we were going to meet a real dragon, I was *so* frightened I got hiccups. We were having breakfast, and Queen Gloriana and Fairy G. came in to say good morning.

"Good morning, my dear young princesses," Queen Gloriana said.

"I have a very important announcement for the first-year students. This morning, as you know, you have a Creative Cake Cooking for Perfect Palace Parties Class. This afternoon, however, you are to go straight to the Tower Room just as soon as you've finished lunch. You are very fortunate—King Percival has agreed to bring in one of his dragons!"

The room was so quiet, you could have heard a pin drop. My heart was beating so fast, I thought I might burst. Then I hiccuped. And I was so embarrassed!

"Now," our principal went on, "I want you all to listen very carefully to what King Percival tells you. He will instruct you on How to Talk to Dragons, and he will give you your tiara points at the end of the lesson. I look forward to hearing that you all have at least ten points!" And then she swept out of the dining hall, and Fairy G.—who is much too huge to sweep out of anything—stomped out after her.

Of course we all started to talk at once, except for Princess Perfecta and Princess Floreen. Perfecta pretended to give a bored yawn, and Floreen immediately copied her. Just because Perfecta was at the Academy last year, she thinks she knows *everything*, even though she only got about a hundred tiara points in the whole year! Princess Alice's sister said Queen Gloriana was furious with Perfecta, and now she's back in the first year with us.

"A dragon!" Princess Katie said. Her eyes were shining. "What fun!"

"Do you think it'll be very big?"

I asked nervously.

"Huge and ferocious!" Princess Charlotte said.

Princess Sophia shook her head. "Queen Gloriana would never allow that," she said. "I bet it'll be a very old dragon that can't even

breathe fire anymore."

"Come on!" Alice stood up. "Let's go and get the boring old Cake Cooking Class over with. Then we can see the dragon for real! Hurry up and finish your toast, Daisy."

I looked at the toast lying untouched on my plate. I didn't feel very hungry—especially when I saw the burnt edges. They made me think of fiery breath.

"I'm done, thank you," I said.

Princess Emily took my hand as we hurried out of the dining room. "Don't worry," she whispered. "It'll be okay. At least, I hope so!"

Behind us, Princess Perfecta said loudly, "Some people are *such* scaredy-cats!"

Chapter Two

Our cooking lesson was a disaster! Usually I enjoy cooking classes, because when I'm at home our cook won't let me near the kitchen. She says it's not the place for princesses, and chases me away with a big wooden spoon. Luckily,

Queen Gloriana thinks we *should* know how to cook, just in case we don't live happily ever after. She also says that some royal families can't afford cooks.

Anyway, I was so busy worrying about the dragon that I didn't hear when Lady Victoria told us what temperature we should set the oven to. My fairy cakes came out totally black.

Floreen said loudly, "Who needs the fire company now?" She and Perfecta sniggered together.

"Don't pay any attention to her," Sophia said. "Here . . . you can have some of mine."

Katie looked at my baking sheet and giggled. "They look like lumps of coal!" she said. "Throw them away quickly before Lady V. sees them—she'll throw a fit!"

Katie was right. They *did* look like coal, and I couldn't help giggling myself as I looked around for the garbage can. I couldn't find it, so I dropped my poor little cakes into my schoolbag just as Lady V. tiptoed over to us. But we heard her. She wears very high heels!

We tried to look innocent as Lady V. peered over her glasses at our baking sheets.

"Not *quite* as nice as I'd hoped," she said. "Daisy dear, let me try yours!" She picked up one of my cakes (of course, it was really one of Sophia's) and nibbled at it.

TWO

"Oh, no!" she exclaimed. "You used salt instead of sugar! Oh, dear me. I can't give a single one of you any tiara points. What disappointing little cooks you are!

I was hoping your fairy cakes would be the pride of King Percival's Celebration Party tonight."

Floreen sat up at once. You could almost see her ears perk up. "A *party*, Lady Victoria?"

Lady V. waved a dismissive hand. "For King Percival's *special* friends only, Princess Floreen. Lots of fireworks and dancing in the moonlight on the roof terrace of his wonderful palace." She looked at us sadly. "I'd planned on presenting him with a mountain of fairy cakes with pearly pink icing."

"Please, Lady Victoria—*my* fairy cakes are just right!" Perfecta called out, and under her breath she muttered, "And I didn't cheat like scaredy-cat Daisy!"

Lady V. shook her head. "No, Perfecta dear. Yours are a teensy bit undercooked. And please take two *minus* tiara points for calling

out so boastfully."

Perfecta scowled as Lady V. tiptoed away. Then the bell rang loudly, and we all trooped out into the hallway and headed for lunch.

I couldn't eat any of my pizza. I kept thinking I could smell

smoke, and it made me twitchy. Emily didn't eat much either.

"The dragon will be chained up, won't it?" she asked Alice.

Alice rubbed her nose. "I don't know. When my big sister was here, she never met a real dragon. King Percival was supposed to bring one in, but the dragon was sick or having a baby or something, and he brought in a cardboard one instead. My sister was *really* disappointed!"

"Oh," Emily said in a very small voice.

Knowing Emily was anxious made me feel a bit braver. "We'll stick together," I said.

"Scaredy-cats!" hissed Floreen. Perfecta laughed.

"We'll *all* stay together," Sophia said firmly.

Emily and I held hands tightly as we tiptoed up the stairs toward the

Tower Room. It's usually my favorite room—it's got a huge window that opens on to the Academy roof, and you can see for miles and miles and miles—but this time I went up the stairs really slowly.

voice was shaky. "But we *are* princesses . . ."

I swallowed hard. "Yes," I said. "Let's go!"

And in we went, expecting to see a huge dragon with glittering scales and ferocious glaring eyes. I was ready to run away if it was too terrible . . .

. . . But it wasn't terrible at all.

The dragon was totally fantastic!

Sophia and Alice were holding hands as well, and even Charlotte and Katie hesitated before they went through the doorway.

"Oooooh!" I said nervously. "I'm—I'm scared, Emily!"

"Me too," Emily said, and her

Tower Room. It's usually my favorite room—it's got a huge window that opens on to the Academy roof, and you can see for miles and miles and miles—but this time I went up the stairs really slowly.

"Scaredy-cats!" hissed Floreen. Perfecta laughed.

"We'll *all* stay together," Sophia said firmly.

Emily and I held hands tightly as we tiptoed up the stairs toward the

Chapter Three

$\mathcal{A}$lice, Katie, Sophia, Charlotte, and the rest of the first-year princesses were already making little "Ooooh!" and "Aaaah!" noises, and I could see why. It was just a baby, with shimmery scales on its fat silver stomach and the sweetest tiny green wings.

It was gazing at us with huge golden eyes, and it truly looked as if the poor little thing was scared of *us*!

King Percival was standing behind the little dragon, and he was actually smiling! King P.'s about a hundred years old, and very fat and whiskery. He normally frowns a lot—especially when we get things wrong when he teaches our How to Be Polite to Princes Class (we are *so* not good at that!). But this time he was looking very pleased and proud.

"Ha!" he said. "Cute little beast, isn't he? Gotta get him trained, of course, but he's doing fine. Want to tickle his ears? Sort of thing you girls like doing, after all. Good introduction to dragons too. You'll never be afraid of the big ones once you've met a little one."

I could see Katie's eyes sparkle. "Can we really?" she asked. "He's *so* beautiful."

King P. puffed out his stomach, as if he was the proud father. "I suppose he *is* a bit of a stunner," he said. "Now, move slowly. We don't want to scare him."

Katie and Charlotte tiptoed toward the little dragon, and while Katie tickled his ears Charlotte scratched him under his chin. He made a funny little purring noise, and you could see he really liked it.

"That's good, girls," King P. said.

"I'm glad to see you're not afraid of the little guy. Next!"

He looked straight at me, but

before I could say anything, Perfecta raised her hand.

"You'll have to excuse Princess Daisy, Your Majesty," she said in a nasty, sneery voice. "She's *petrified* of dragons!"

"No, I'm *not*!" I said. I was

furious! That little dragon was so cute I was *dying* to hold him. I glared at Perfecta and took a step forward, and at exactly that moment, Floreen put out her foot. I tripped and fell with a huge *crash*.

The dragon let out a wail and dashed for the window—and before any of us could move, he'd smashed through the glass and was scampering around on a flat part of the roof outside.

And then the most incredibly scary thing happened! There was a humongous roar, and a giant puff of smoke—and the most enormous dragon you could ever imagine came flying up from somewhere down below. Her scales glittered and shone, and as she turned and twisted in the air, her massive leathery wings beat up and down with a *thwump! thwump!*

sound. Her huge golden eyes were angry, and as we stood frozen to the floor, a blast of flame shot past the broken Tower Room window. We could actually hear the glass

sizzling as it melted!

And then King Percival did something incredibly brave. He ran straight to the gaping hole where the red-hot glass was still dripping, and began blowing and blowing into a silver whistle around his neck . . .

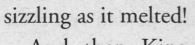

. . . And the dragon stopped in midair and hovered there, staring in at him!

It was *amazing*!

"*Down!*" King Percival shouted in a voice like a foghorn. "Bad dragon. Down! At once! Argent, go down to earth!"

The enormous dragon blinked,

and all of a sudden she didn't look so scary. She circled and then dropped down until she was out of sight. A moment later, she was gone, and only the smell of smoke was left hanging in the air. And the little dragon was still crouched outside on the flat roof. He was squeaking miserably as he called for his mother.

King Percival mopped his forehead as he turned to where we were all standing. Our eyes were totally popping out of our heads.

"Ha!" he said. "Everyone all right? Nobody burnt to cinders?"

I don't think any of us could

speak, we were so surprised by what had happened—but it was strange. Although the dragon had been so gigantic and totally extraordinary, there was something about the way she'd looked at King P. that reminded me of the way my dog looked when he knew he'd been bad. Somehow I didn't feel scared anymore. Not at all!

"Good. Good. Glad to hear it. Um, sorry if Argent popped up a bit suddenly. She was worried about her baby, I expect. Quite understandable, really. We'll bring the little fellow in and take him back—"

King P. suddenly stopped. He stared out the window, and so did we.

The little dragon had crept to the far end of the roof and was balanced on the top of a tall chimney.

"Oh, no!" Alice whispered. "How ever did he get there?"

"He must have scrambled up somehow," King P. said. "He can't fly yet. He might have been looking for soot. He's always hungry."

King Percival walked over to what used to be the window and peered out. "Come along, little fella!" he called. "Down you come! Come along!"

But the baby dragon wouldn't move. King P. called and whistled, but he wouldn't budge.

"Can't his mother fly up and get him, Your Majesty?" Charlotte suggested.

King P. shook his head. "Can't risk it, my dear. She's a good old dragon—one of the best—but she's clumsy. She'd have that chimney top rolling down the roof with one beat of her wings."

He sighed heavily. "I wish I knew what to do. Never even *thought* to bring a bag of coal with me. Oh well. I guess I'd better go and ask Fairy G. for help. You girls can go now. There's no point in staying here."

"Excuse me, Your Majesty, but shouldn't we stay and make sure the little dragon doesn't move?" Sophia asked.

I was glad she'd suggested it. I don't think any of us wanted to leave him there all on his own.

King P. pulled at his beard. "Hmm. It might be useful. But *don't* go near the window. Understand?"

"Yes, Your Majesty," we chorused.

Chapter Four

We broke up into little groups as King P. went puffing down the stairs. Of course, Katie and Charlotte came hurrying over to where Emily, Alice, Sophia, and I were standing.

"Did you ever imagine we'd have

a lesson like this?" Katie asked, her eyes shining.

"Never!" I said. "I hope that little dragon will be okay."

"That's some lesson!" Perfecta said spitefully, as she barged up beside us. "Because it's *all* your fault, scaredy-cat Daisy. If you hadn't frightened that dragon, he'd never have run away!"

"That's right," Floreen agreed. "You'll probably be expelled when Queen Gloriana finds out!"

"No, she won't," Emily said. "It wasn't her fault she slipped!"

"I *didn't* slip," I began, and then I stopped. Emily had been right there when Floreen tripped me, and if she hadn't noticed, who else would have? If I explained, it would just sound as if I was making up excuses.

"Don't worry, Daisy," Sophia said. "Anyone with any sense could see it was an accident."

I know she meant well, but I began to feel really terrible.

Especially when Charlotte said, "We'll tell everyone you didn't mean to scare him."

Perfecta smiled her sneery smile. "We knew you were going to scare him as soon as you rushed at him, didn't we, Floreen?"

Floreen nodded. "Trying to pretend you were brave!"

"Daisy *is* brave," Emily said. "It's much more brave to do something when you're scared than when you don't care!"

That made me feel even worse—because I hadn't been scared. I'd been *angry*—angry with Perfecta.

And then a totally awful thought hit me. *What if Perfecta was right? Had I scared the little dragon before Floreen tripped me?* I was so confused I didn't know what to think, and then a huge voice boomed from the doorway, and my knees turned to jelly.

"Could somebody tell me *exactly* what's been going on in this classroom?"

Fairy G. was standing in the doorway, and she was so mad she'd grown to twice her usual size. As I raised my hand, I was more frightened than I ever could have been of any dragon.

I don't know how I got to the end of my explanation, but I did. Fairy G. didn't say anything while I stuttered and mumbled, but I was sure she thought I was terrible. When I'd finished, she told me to stay where I was. Everybody else was instructed to go straight to the dining room.

"Please, Fairy G.," Katie said bravely. "King Percival asked us to look after the dragon while he got help."

"I will see to that!" Fairy G. boomed.

As soon as everyone else had left, Fairy G. gave me a piercing stare.

"Now, Princess Daisy! I'm going to leave you here while I go and see if I can find a sack of coal for poor King Percival. He's tearing his whiskers out with worry about that bad little dragon, but he seems to think it'll come down soon enough if it gets something to eat. And as you've told me it was you that scared it away, you can wait here and watch it until I get back."

I noticed that Fairy G. was more her normal size as she stomped off, and I wondered if I would ever get used to the way she grew and shrank. I also wondered if I'd totally imagined the very tiny wink I'd seen as she turned around for a moment in the doorway.

Chapter Five

"Daisy!"

I whirled around and saw Emily, Katie, Alice, Charlotte, and Sophia tiptoeing into the room.

"What are you doing here?" I gasped. "You'll be in a lot of trouble if Fairy G. finds you! You'll get thousands of minus tiara points!"

"We couldn't leave you on your own," Alice said. "And we had a great idea. Look! We've brought our fairy cakes! We thought the dragon might be hungry." She waved a bag at me.

"I keep telling her he won't like them," Sophia said. "King Percival said he liked coal, but we couldn't find any."

"At least we can try," Alice told her.

I stared at them both. Something was whizzing around in my brain—and then I remembered! *My* cakes—my *burnt* cakes . . . Where were they?

I dashed to my bag and pulled it open. Yes! They were still there. And they *did* look like lumps of coal!

"Look!" I said, and I threw one out of the window. It was much too light to throw very far. It dropped a long way from the chimney—but the little dragon noticed! He sat up and licked his lips!

"He likes them!" Katie laughed.

"Try and get them nearer," Charlotte suggested.

"Yes," I said. "Yes." And I took a deep breath, picked up my bag, and climbed out of the window and onto the roof.

"Daisy! Come back!" Emily yelled. "That's too dangerous!"

I didn't pay any attention. I walked steadily toward the little dragon, and, as I got nearer, I began to talk to him in a soothing kind of way. When he started to look anxious, I stopped and put two cakes down on the roof.

"There," I said, "there . . ." Then

I walked away just as slowly as I'd come, dropping a trail of burnt crumbs behind me.

I heard the little dragon jump down before I even reached the window, and I could tell by looking at my friends' faces that he was following me.

Katie was beckoning me. Sophia was smiling, and Emily was nodding. Alice and Charlotte were quietly clapping. I climbed back into the tower and trailed more crumbs into the center of the room until the bag was empty. Then we all moved right back against the

walls, and held our breath.

Pitter-patter . . . pitter-patter . . . and he was inside!

By the time Fairy G. came back up the stairs with King Percival and a page boy carrying a sack of coal, the baby dragon was happily chewing my fairy cakes. I was scratching his ears, and he was purring.

First King P. looked amazed, then extremely happy.

"Good boy!" he said, and I thought I could see a tear in his eye. "Oh, what a good boy!"

"Daisy persuaded him to come

back," Emily said. "She did it all by herself!"

Fairy G. gave me a huge smile. "And I thought you were afraid of dragons!"

"Not anymore," I said. It was true.

And that was the end of our dragon lesson—except for a very very special invitation from King Percival asking all six of us to go to his celebration party!

King Percival
cordially invites you
to a
Celebration Party
Tonight on the roof terrace of his palace
Starts 6:30 pm

"I owe you girls a great big thank you," he said in his gruff old voice.

"Hmph!" said Fairy G. She was busy repairing the window with her wand, but it wasn't a bad kind of "Hmph." "Do they *really* deserve a treat after all the trouble they've caused?"

"Trouble?" asked King P.

"Tell him, Daisy," Fairy G. said, but she was twinkling as she said it.

"It was my fault the baby was scared, Your Majesty," I said. "And I'm *truly* sorry."

"Nonsense, my dear!" King P.

shook his head. "I saw it all. You were tripped! I've just been telling Fairy G. That Floreen girl stuck out her foot, and so I've given her twenty minus tiara points. I've given you plus points, of course. All six of you. Thirty tiara points each!"

And I'm sure it's very unprincessy of me, but I couldn't help being just a little bit pleased.

Chapter Six

The party was in honor of the baby dragon's first birthday. The truly wonderful *wonderful* thing was that we got to go to King Percival's palace by flying on a dragon! Argent, the baby's mother, was so big that we could all sit on her scaly

back—and she flew us all the way.
Oh, it was so much fun! Fireworks
whooshed and *sizzled* and *banged*,
and showers of beautiful
sparkly rainbow stars
showered down from
rockets as we danced and

danced on the magical rooftop.

When the last fireworks finally died away, Argent flew up into the air and blew fiery smoke rings

that floated gently down to the ground. Then the moon came out, and we danced some more below the silver moonbeams.

I don't really remember flying home. I think I was too sleepy.

And I don't know if I dreamed that Fairy G. tucked me into bed when we got back, but I'm sure I heard her say, "Good night, Rose Room Princesses! Good night!"

What happens next?

FIND OUT IN

Princess Alice
∽ AND THE ∾
Magical Mirror

Hi! I've been dying to meet you—you're the best! Not like horrible Princess Perfecta and nasty Princess Floreen. Sometimes they're so spiteful. My big sister says it's because Perfecta didn't earn enough tiara points to join the Tiara Club last year, so now she's back in the first year with us. Poor us!

I'm Princess Alice, by the way. I'm learning to be a Perfect Princess at the Princess Academy, just like you. But you know what school is like—hard work! If it weren't for Charlotte, Katie, Emily, Daisy, and Sophia, I think I'd collapse. And I don't know about you, but I just can't be good all the time. . . .

You are cordially invited to visit www.tiaraclubbooks.com!

Visit your special princess friends at their dazzling website!

Find the secret word hidden in each of the first six Tiara Club books. Then go to the Tiara Club website, enter the secret word, and get an exclusive poster. Print out the poster for each book and save it. When you have all six, put them together to make one amazing poster of the entire Royal Princess Academy. Use the stickers in the books to decorate and make your very own perfect princess academy poster.

More fun at www.tiaraclubbooks.com:

- Download your own Tiara Club membership card!

- Win future Tiara Club books.

- Get activities and coloring sheets with every new book.

- Stay up-to-date with the princesses in this great series!

Visit www.tiaraclubbooks.com and be a part of the Tiara Club!